To Fred

First published in 2017 by Child's Play (International) Ltd
Ashworth Road, Bridgemead, Swindon SN5 7YD, UK

First published in USA in 2018 by Child's Play Inc
250 Minot Avenue, Auburn, Maine 04210

Distributed in Australia by Child's Play Australia Pty Ltd
Unit 10/20 Narabang Way, Belrose, Sydney, NSW 2085

ISBN 978-1-78628-003-9
CLP160817CPL10170039

Printed in Shenzhen, China

1 3 5 7 9 10 8 6 4 2

A catalogue record of this book
is available from the British Library

www.childs-play.com

The
BIG RED ROCK

Jess Stockham

One day, Bif was so busy eating his breakfast...

that he didn't notice
the Big Red Rock,

until...

Then Bif remembered his manners, and asked the rock nicely.

out of my way

please;

pretty

please,

please!

But the Big Red Rock didn't move.

So Bif tried
to kick it...

and bash it...

and push it...

push!
shove!

and pester it out of his way.

burn!

But the
Big Red Rock
stayed exactly
where it was.

Bif was wondering what to do next when Bop turned up.

"Can you move big red rocks?" asked Bif. "This one is in my way."

"I can't," said Bop. "But I might know someone who can." And he ran off.

"Meet the Big Red Rock Eater!"
said Bop when he returned.
"She may be able to help!"

But the Big Red Rock Eater had a wobbly tooth. She could only nibble small pieces!

So Bop ran off to find
someone else who could help.

"Meet the Small Blue Rock Singer!" said Bop when he came back. "His voice is so loud it can break rocks!"

But the Big Red Rock stayed in one piece.
So Bop ran off again to find some more help.

This time he returned with
the Yellow Rock Crusher...

and the Green Rock Driller.

Then he fetched the Orange Rock Scarer...

the Pink Rock Sucker...

But nothing could move the Big Red Rock!

It was NEVER going to move... EVER!

"It's just a silly Big Red Rock that will NEVER, EVER move!" cried Bif. "Let's leave it alone and go and play!"

dance!

So they did...

shake!

until somehow...

...only to find
a Big Red Rock
was in his way!

ROCK
CRUSHER

Rock Singer

rock
SCARER rocks

ROCK

Bif
was here

THE ROCK TICKLER WAS HERE

EATER

THE ROCK DRILLER drills ok

the Rock sucker

Bop